THE FART BOOK

Ivory Tower edition licensed from Once Upon a Planet Inc.

WRITTEN BY DONALD WETZEL
ILLUSTRATED BY MARTIN RISKIN

COPYRIGHT 1992

IVORY TOWER **PUBLISHING COMPANY INCORPORATED**

PUBLISHED SIMULTANEOUSLY IN CANADA BY MARKA CANADA ETOBICOKE, ONTARIO M9W 5Z6

DISTRIBUTED IN AUSTRALIA BY ABALNON PTY. LTD. CONCORD WEST, N.S.W. 2138

DISTRIBUTED IN THE UNITED KINGDOM BY

WHYNOT PRODUCTIONS LTD. EAST SUSSEX TN21 OXL

DISTRIBUTED IN NEW ZEALAND BY BLACKWOOD GAYLE DISTRIBUTORS AUCKLAND.

38

39 40 41 42 43 44 45 46

47 48 49 50

IVORY TOWER PUBLSHING COMPANY, INC.
125 WALNUT STREET, WATERTOWN, MA 02172
TEL#: (617) 923-1111
FAX: (617) 923-8839

INTRO-
DUCTION

To the best of my knowledge there has been no full length work attempted on the subject of farts. Which is hard to figure, as everyone on earth that lives and breathes also farts. Even the president. He farts oval farts. Due to the office. When my dad worked in an office he used to call it the orifice. I like puns but I do not think they belong in a book such as this. Otherwise I would have said that the president farts oval farts due to his orifice. Which would have been the best pun I ever thought of.

Note To Readers

All farts are divided into two groups.

    1. Your farts

    2. Somebody else's farts.

There are some farts that can only be positively identified when they are your own, such as the different kinds of silent or near silent farts. Odor alone will not always do. There is a feel to some farts that is necessary to their identification and naturally only the farter gets the feeling.

In case of doubt I will try and make clear which of the two groups each fart is apt to be found in. But the reader is asked to keep this in mind for himself when using this guide to avoid unnecessary confusion and false identifications.

All the farts in this book will be arranged alphabetically. If a person knows their alphabet they should have no trouble understanding this arrangement or figuring things out.

THE ALARM FART

This is a good fart for the beginner. It is easy to identify. It starts with a loud unnaturally high note, wavers like a siren, and ends with a quick downward note that stops before you expect it to. It sounds like something is wrong. If it happens to you you will know right off why it is called the Alarm Fart. You will be alarmed. The Alarm Fart however is rare.

THE AMPLIFIED FART

This is any fart that gets its power more from being amplified than from the fart itself. A metal porch swing will amplify a fart every time. So will a plywood table, an empty fifty gallon drum, a tin roof, or some empty cardboard boxes if they are strong enough to sit on. Any fart made a great deal louder than it really is through being amplified in this way can be called an Amplified Fart. These are common farts under the right conditions.

THE BATHTUB FART

People who would never in their life know one fart from another, who would like to act like farts don't exist, will have to admit that a Bathtub Fart is something special.

It is the only fart you can see!

What you see is the bubble or bubbles.

The Bathtub Fart can be either single or multiple noted and fair or foul as to odor. It makes no difference. The farter's location is what does it.

Maybe there is a kind of muffled pong and one big bubble. Or there may be a ping ping ping and a bunch of bubbles.

The sound I should point out depends somewhat on the depth of the water and even more on the tub. If it is one of those big old heavy tubs with the funny legs you can get terrific sound effects. While one of the new thin ones half buried in the floor can be disappointing.

But either way, as long as the water is deep enough, whatever the sound, up comes the bubble or bubbles and you have to be quick but glance back over your shoulder and you have seen it, the Bathtub Fart, the most positively identifiable fart known to man.

It is a common fart and strictly group one unless you are a kid still young enough to take baths with your friends.

5

THE BIGGEST FART IN THE WORLD FART

Like the great bald eagle, this fart is pretty well described just by its name. This can either be a group one or a group two fart and can occur just about anywhere. I heard it one time, a group two identification, in a crowded high school auditorium one night, right in that silence that happens when a room full of people has stopped singing the Star Spangled Banner and sat down. It came from the back. There was not a soul in that room that missed it. A fart like that can be impressive.

The most diagnostic characteristic of the Biggest Fart In The World is its size. Fart freaks who go around showing off, farting like popcorn machines and making faces before they fart or asking you to pull their finger and then they fart, never have what it takes for this one, which is rare even among your most serious farters.

THE BURNING BRAKES FART

A silent fart identified by odor alone. Usually an adult fart, occurring while the adult is driving a car or has a front seat passenger who farts. The Burning Brakes Fart actually does smell a little like burning brakes and seems to hang around longer than most farts. Which gives whoever farted a chance to make a big show of checking to see if the emergency brake has been left on. When he finds it hasn't you know who farted. A common automobile fart.

THE CAR DOOR FART

Either a group one or a group two fart. Very tricky. It is meant to be a concealed fart. A matter of close timing is involved, the farter trying to fart at the exact moment he slams the car door shut. It is usually a good loud fart. It is one of the funnier farts when it doesn't work, which is almost every time. It is a desperation fart and not too common.

THE CELESTIAL FART

Not to be confused with the Did An Angel Speak Fart, which is simply any loud fart in church. The Celestial Fart is soft and delicate, surprising in a boy or an adult. It is probably the most shy of all farts and might be compared with the wood thrush, a very shy bird. It does not have the sly or cunning sound of the Whisper Fart. It is just a very small clear fart with no odor at all. Very rare.

THE CHINESE FIRECRACKER FART

This is an exceptional multiple noted fart identified by the number and variety of its noises, mostly pops and bangs. Often when you think it is all over it still has a few pops and bangs to go. In friendly company this one can get applause. Uncommon.

THE CROWD FART

The Crowd Fart is distinguished by its very potent odor, strong enough to make quite a few people look around. The trick here is not to identify the fart but the farter. This is almost impossible unless the farter panics and starts a fit of coughing or starts staring at the ceiling or the sky as though something up there fascinates him. In which case he is the one. Very common.

THE DID AN ANGEL SPEAK FART

This is any loud fart in church. This fart was first called to my attention by my father. He probably read about it somewhere. For fart watchers who go to church, this is a good one to watch for as this is the only place it can be found.

THE DOG DID IT FART

It is necessary for a dog to be around for this fart to occur. People who fart and blame it on the dog when there is no dog within miles are making a travesty of the whole fart identification business, which is difficult enough as it is. This is always a silent fart but one with an odor you could blame on a dog that was dead. The farter tries to blame it on the dog. He will even go so far as to run the dog out of the house. Do not be fooled. When a dog farts it will usually grunt too. It may even get up and walk away. This is what you should do when you have identified a Dog Did It Fart. They are vile.

THE DRUM ROLL FART

Some people might want to put this fart under the general heading of Musical Farts (see under M) but I for one have never considered the drum very much of a musical instrument. It is a multiple noted fart of the same tone or pitch farted very fast. It sounds more like a real drum roll when now and then the farter happens to throw in a rim shot at the end, but you can not expect this every time. It should in no way be confused with the Chinese Firecracker Fart, which is by far the more colorful of the two, although the Drum Roll Fart is much more rare.

THE ENGLISH FART

A very classy fart. The sound alone distinguishes it from all other farts. There are some who will say that this is a put-on accent, but that is silly. When it comes to farting no one goes around sounding like an Englishman. It happens or it doesn't. The sound it makes is, *thip.* Sometimes it will go *thip, thip.* It is unmistakable. It is probably as proper and upper class as a fart can get.

THE EXCLAMATION FART

This is a punctuation fart. Timing is the whole thing. The farter, or some-one, must be speaking. For instance, the speaker will say, "Ah, shut up!" and then someone will fart a loud sharp fart. This is a true Exclamation Fart. If the speaker is also the farter he may delay his fart until the right moment and then force it for all he is worth. If it works it is still a true Exclamation Fart, although more often than not it is an accident and for this reason rare.

THE EXECUTIVE FART

A very loud clear fart by a very important person is an Executive Fart. It is either sharp or flat, somewhat off key, but otherwise a very business-like fart. No nonsense about it. But no one is supposed to notice. Particularly the farter. If you do not laugh at the Executive Fart this is either because you are scared of the person who farted or because the fart is so gross. Common with very important people.

THE FIRE FART

There is probably no other fart about which there is more confusion or which has as many other common names. It has been called the Scorcher Fart, the Burning Britches Fart, the Solar Fart, the Natural Gas or Front Burner Fart and other names. But its correct name is simply the Fire Fart. It is called this because of the sensation it gives the farter when he farts. It burns.

For this reason it is mostly a group one identification fart. People can make all kinds of faces when they fart. A look of pain when a person farts does not necessarily mean they have farted a Fire Fart. Some people look pained when they fart any kind of fart at all.

But as a group one fart there is never any question about it at all. You will wonder sometimes if it smokes. The only way this can be a group two identification is if it is confirmed. You have to say to the one who farted, "Did that fart burn?" If they say yes, you have identified and confirmed a group two identification Fire Fart. This will not happen very often.

But this can also lead into the question of whether farts actually burn or not. If you say to someone who has farted, "Did that fart burn?" they are apt to try and turn the subject away from themselves and start an argument. "Farts don't burn, you dummy," they will say. Then if you say that as a matter of fact a fart will too burn, they will argue back that while a fart is gas it is not the kind of gas that burns, or that there is not enough gas in a fart to burn, or that you are weird. I have seen people who know nothing about the subject at all get quite hot about it.

Anyone who does not believe that a fart will burn, should check it out with Joe Brantly, who is by now pretty well known throughout all of Baldwin County Alabama as Blue Flame Brantly. Try and tell him that a fart won't burn.

He has stopped trying to deny it. There were witnesses. About ten of them.

The way it happened was this. Blue Flame Brantly is a big football player with a very hairy ass. A nice guy they say. Easy going. So one day after football practice the team was back in the locker room and Blue Flame Brantly had just got out of the shower (only he was known as just Joe Brantly then) and was drying himself off and some wise guy wondered if the hairs around his ass would burn, wet as they were. Joe had one foot up on the bench and was bent over looking at a bad case of athlete's foot he had and this wise guy sneaked up behind him with a cigarette lighter. They say that Joe should have noticed how quiet it got right then in the locker room, but he didn't.

He was bent way over looking at his athlete's foot. Worried about it probably. Anyhow, with all those people watching, just as the kid clicked his lighter and it lit, Joe Brantly farted a big one. And it burned. Ten people or more saw a long blue flame shoot back at least three inches from his ass.

I was not there myself. But I have talked to some that were, and they swear it happened. Not only did the fart burn with a long blue flame, but it caught the hair around his ass on fire and he had to beat it with a towel to put it out.

There may still be some people who believe that a fart will not burn, despite this true account. I could tell them to go ahead and test it for themselves, but due to the danger it is probably best to stick to identifying the Fire Fart as a group one fart only and to let it go at that.

THE FIZZLE FART

A very wet fart. The sound is *f-z-z-z-z* or *f-s-s-s-s*. It is almost a fart that fails, but not quite. There is an old saying, kind of a rhyme, which I have never heard all the way through, but it is about an old lady who "...farts and fizzles and rots her pants..." The fizzle mentioned here is the Fizzle Fart we are talking about. It is not always an old lady's fart, but it is always on the damp side and sounds like it. This is a common fart with senior citizens and people who eat fast foods.

THE FRENCH FART

Said to be the most beautiful of farts. Usually in a minor key. Soft and musical with many half-tones. Any long drawn out fart that seems beautiful to you is most likely a French Fart. Very rare.

THE GERMAN FART

If you hear a fart that makes you think of a dog it is probably the German Fart. It has either a deep growling or a low barking noise, or both. It comes from deep inside and never seems to get all the way out. Still it can be loud and frightening to small children. The odor varies, but not much, as it is one of the rank ones every time.

THE GIRLS DON'T FART FART

Any fart by a girl. A girl can fart a fart that will shake the walls or blow little birds right out of their nests, but the girl will never give a sign. You are supposed to ignore it. It may be hard to do, but you better do it. With girls this is the most common fart there is.

THE GOING UP STAIRS FART

Aone in a million fart and one of my favorites. This fart breaks on each step as the farter goes up a short flight of steps. Not a step is missed when it is a true Going Up Stairs Fart. It is probably caused by being a hold back fart and the action of going up some stairs cuts it loose. If the fart goes up a note with each step you have the Musical Going Up Stairs Fart. There is no fart more rare than this one.

THE HAIR-TRIGGER FART

Another fart that hardly needs to be described. There is no one that lives and farts that does not know from experience what this fart is like. There is no sign it is on its way. Suddenly it is there. Just barely held back. Like a sneeze about to be sneezed. You know that any movement at all, even a thought, could set it off. And sure enough that is what will happen. A group one identification only. Very common.

THE HARD-BOILED EGG FART

Odor alone identifies this fart. It stinks of sulfur. Due to the sulfur content of hard-boiled eggs. While it is true that powdered sulfur will keep redbugs away when you are out in the woods it is not true that a few Hard-boiled Egg Farts in the evening will keep a whole camp site free of redbugs for the rest of the night. What it may do is keep the camp site free of other campers for the rest of the night.

THE HARVARD FART

The Harvard Fart is different from the English Fart in two ways. First, the sound is different. More of a *thap* sound than a *thip*. The other difference is the way the farter acts about it. With the English Fart, the farter always acts as though nothing has happened. But a person who farts a Harvard Fart will give a sign. He will smile. Or nod. As if he has just heard from God.

THE INCENSE FART

A potent fart. Do not be fooled by its name. It is only called the Incense Fart to be sarcastic. What happens is that someone farts in a crowd. A vile one. Since it cannot be ignored someone will say, "Ah, how lovely; Sandalwood? Jasmine? Gardenia?" Or whatever your favorite incense may be.

THE INTERROGATORY FART

This is a fart that seems to ask a question. Ends on an up note. Seems to say, "Oh?" or, "Well?" It can be a very silly fart when you are alone. As though you are having a conversation with your own ass. Fairly common.

THE INSPIRATIONAL FART

The sound of this fart may best be described as like organ music. However, in my opinion only someone really into farts would actually find this fart inspiring. Still, a sound like organ music is quite a fart, and if it actually gives you goose-flesh at the time it is probably safe to put it down as the Inspirational Fart. Rare.

THE **JUBILATION FART**

Generally the Jubilation Fart can not be told safely from an Inspirational Fart except by an expert. Both farts are hard to believe. Like the hippopotamus and the rhinoceros. In the short time a fart lasts it is always hard to make up your mind which one it is. If you suddenly saw a hippopotamus or a rhinoceros for as short a time you would probably have the same trouble. The rhinoceros is the one with the horn at the end of its nose.

THE **JUNK FART**

This is a fart that we could just as well do without. It comes from eating junk and it sounds like it. A *pish-whish* sound. Like a swinging door. As farts go there is really nothing to it. It comes chiefly from eating at a fast food restaurant. It can happen while you are still there. Still eating. It's that quick. In and out, no waiting. The same as the service they advertise. This fart is way too common.

THE KAMIKAZE FART

Sometimes called the Suicide Fart or the Killer Fart. Kamikaze is the correct name. (Kamikaze means divine wind. For a fact.) It wipes out everybody. The farter in every case will have a crazy look about him. This is one of the ways this fart can be identified. The farter will be wiped out too. Any person who farts a Kamikaze Fart and brags about it is a fart fanatic and probably dangerous in other ways.

THE KINKY FART

A person who farts while kissing another person has farted a Kinky Fart. This is a rotten thing to do.

THE KIPLING FART

The origin of this fart is interesting, if true. It was supposed to have happened at the University of South Alabama. What happened was that a strange professor was talking to another professor one day who happened to be a great one for making jokes and the strange professor said, "Do you like Kipling?" And the joker said, "I don't know. How do you kiple?" And the strange professor said, "Like this." And then he farted. This fart has a *kiple* sound.

THE LISP FART

This is a fart that is funny in any situation. Even alone. It is simply a fart that lisps. You will know it when you hear it. It can be particularly funny, a group two identification, when the farter happens to be someone who also lisps when they talk.

THE LOOSE BOARD FART

The Loose Board Fart has to sound squeaky, like a loose board you have just stepped on. Some people call just any fart a Loose Board Fart. Just to have something to say. These are the same sort of people who say the dog did it when there is no dog in sight. Listen for the squeaky, creaky sound.

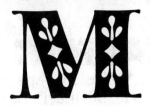

THE MUD SUCKER FART

The most gross sounding of all farts. It sounds like someone with his foot stuck in the mud slowly pulling it out. Identification is positive by sound alone. No other fart makes a wet sucking noise. Fairly common with tootsie roll eaters.

SQUOINK!

THE MUSICAL FART

This is a special category. All Musical Farts do not necessarily sound musical. This may seem odd, but that is the way it works. Who would think, for instance, that Spanish moss is related to the pineapple? But it is.

All Musical Farts are rare, and identification is often a matter of opinion.

THE CLASSICAL FART

Loud and soft, loud and soft. Goes on when you think it has ended.

THE HARD ROCK FART

A highly amplified musical fart. Can make a dog howl with pain. The farter doesn't care if you like it or not. You may not think it is musical but he does.

THE STAR SPANGLED BANNER FART

This is one of the few farts that can bring tears to people's eyes and lumps to their throats and otherwise get them all stirred up.

THE WA-WA FART

This is not a baby fart. The wa-wa is an electrical gadget worked by a guitar player's foot that makes an electric guitar make weird wa-wa sounds. Not all people would call the sound musical.

THE
NATURAL GAS FART

Another name for the Fire Fart. (See under F.)

THE
OCTAVE FART

Some people would put the Octave Fart under musical farts. This would be a mistake but some will do it anyhow. All small birds that look like warblers are not warblers. Some are vireos. The Octave Fart goes under O. The sound of this fart is one note going up or down a full octave, quick or slow, loud or soft, major or minor. This may be a hard one to identify for a person who does not know what an octave is. Rare.

THE PING-PONG BALL FART

An unusual hollow sounding multiple noted fart. Sound alone is diagnostic. It sounds like a ping-pong ball which has been dropped on a table from several feet up and then bounced until it fell off. There can be quite a wait between bounces. This is probably the most rare of all multiple noted farts.

THE POO-POO FART

This is a fart by a very small kid. The kid farts and then says, "Go poo-poo now." And somebody takes him and he does.

THE PRESIDENT'S FART

This rare fart was described in the introduction to this work. What is rare about this fart is that we are talking about presidents of the United States. There is only one of them at a time and they stay pretty much to themselves. But it is fair to suppose that they fart about as much as anybody else. Get one of these on your list, though, and you have really got one.

THE QUACK-QUACK FART

This is a silly name for a fart. A lot of people will call it the Duck Fart. But it is important to remember that this is a double noted fart. And while quack-quack is the sound a duck makes and the sound of the Quack-Quack Fart, there is nothing to stop a duck from going quack just once, not twice. So that is why it is called the Quack-Quack Fart. Just to be exact. Fairly rare.

THE QUAWONK FART

Somewhat similar to the Quack-Quack Fart. Mostly because of the Q sound. Very few farts have a Q sound. But the Quawonk Fart is single noted and far more soft and pleasant sounding than the Quack-Quack Fart. If you will say quawonk softly to your self, that is the sound.

THE ROVER FART

Commonly called the Dog Fart. However a Dog Fart is actually a fart by a dog. It is beyond the scope of this work to go into all the animal farts. (I have been told that a mule fart can blow down a barn door and that pigs all fart like they are popping bubble gum, but none of this may be true.) Sound is diagnostic in identifying the Rover Fart. Any barking sound will do. Arf arf or ruff ruff or woff woff. Even bow-wow, although a fart that goes bow-wow would be a pretty far out fart.

THE
SCRATCHASS FART

Surprisingly this is the only really dirty name for a fart in this whole work. But it is the right name all right. The action of the farter is diagnostic. He has farted and it itches. He just has to scratch. As a group two identification you have to make certain first that the person scratching his ass has really farted. Some people have a habit of scratching their ass about every five minutes. Common.

THE S'CUSE ME FART

This rare fart excuses itself as it is farted. It is about as close to words as a fart can get. The sound it makes is like a little soft whisper that says, "S'cuse me." The most polite of all farts and very silly when you are alone.

THE STRING OF PEARLS FART

A most unusual and perfect toned fart. Round clear evenly spaced notes. This one is really a beauty. Very rich ladies would like to fart this one every time if they could. Very rare.

THE
TALKING
FART

This unusual fart sounds like it is imitating human speech. About the way a parrot does. Only the Talking Fart does not really say a thing. People will look at you and say, "What?" All you can do is shrug or look dumb.

THE UNMENTIONABLE FART

A tricky one to identify, even though it is probably more common than anyone wants to admit. It all depends on the situation or who farted. I will give some examples. You are alone with your girl friend and she farts. Or you do. It may be loud or rank or both, but either way it is unmentionable. Or you are in the principal's office and there is just the principal and his secretary and you, and you didn't fart but somebody did. Much as you might like to say it wasn't you that did it, you know better. Either the principal or the secretary probably feels the same way. But the other one is very glad that the Unmentionable Fart cannot be mentioned. Or they would lose some Brownie points for sure.

THE VENDING MACHINE FART

Very similar to the Car Door Fart, only here the farter tries to conceal his fart by making a lot of racket getting some gum or candy from a vending machine. He will even pound and kick the machine for some time after it has given him his gum or candy bar, waiting for the fart to happen. This usually doesn't work much better than the Car Door Fart, yet people, kids especially, will keep trying it. More damage is done to vending machines this way than anyone realizes.

THE VOLKSWAGEN FART

Any good strong fart in a Volkswagen in the winter or anyhow with the windows closed is the deadly Volkswagen Fart. It can strangle people. While I am generally in favor of people farting whenever they have to fart, they really should try not to fart in a closed Volkswagen. It would be nice if this were one of the rare farts but it isn't.

THE WHISPER FART

This is an eased out fart that really works. Not everyone can manage it. It takes control. It is one of the most sly and cunning farts there is. You will know the sort of person who is most apt to fart the Whisper Fart. He will be sneaky about everything. This can be a hard one to get on your list.

THE XMAS FART

The Xmas Fart is any ordinary fart that is farted at Christmas. That is the only special thing about it. That and the fact that it is a fart that starts with the letter X. An example of the Xmas Fart happened with me at school. It was not Christmas but the last day of school before Christmas. It happened in Mrs. Schlotsheimer's class. I was sitting at the back of the room right next to Harold Tabor, just the two of us alone. Being so close to Christmas I was sitting there singing Christmas carols in my head and not paying much attention and without thinking I farted a loud one. A regular firecracker. Heads turned all over the room as can be imagined.

I had to think fast.

Hark the herald, I said. And I pointed at Harold.

Everyone thought that he was the one. Harold is crazy about puns but he was not so crazy about that one.

THE YOGA FART

This rare fart is a fart by a person sitting with their legs crossed thinking very heavy thoughts. The chance of a group two identification on this one is pretty slim, as who wants to hang around a person sitting with their legs crossed thinking very heavy thoughts. If it is a group one fart and you are really into Yoga then you should not even notice that you have farted. This could be a tough one to get on your list unless you or your friends are pretty weird.

THE ZIPPER FART

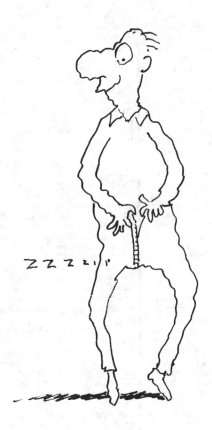

This is the only fart that starts with the letter Z. It goes *Z-z-z-zip.* It hardly sounds like a fart at all. As a matter of fact there may not even be such a fart.

IVORY TOWER PUBLISHING COMPANY INCORPORATED

125 Walnut Street, Watertown, MA 02712

These other fun books are available at many fine stores or by sending $3.50 ea. directly to the publisher.

2000-Do Diapers Give You Leprosy? A humorous look at what every parent should know about bringing up babies.

2015-Games You Can Play With Your Pussy. And lots of other stuff cat owners should know.

2026-Games You Can Play In Bed. A humorous compendium covering everything from Bedtime Bingo to Things To Do at 3:45 A.M.

2034-You Know You're Over Forty When... You Think "Grass" is something to cut and "Getting a little action" means your prune juice is working. A perfect 40th birthday gift.

2042-Cucumbers Are Better Than Men Because... They don't care if you shave your legs, and they never walk around your place when the shades are up. At last, ladies, revenge for all our male chauvinist books.

2061-I'd Rather Be 40 Than Pregnant...Or worrying about getting into graduate school, or travelling with young children, or getting no respect at a ritzy store. Great moral support for women reaching the diaperless age.

2064-The Wedding Night-Facing Nuptial Terrors. For brides and grooms alike: What To Do If He Wants To Take Pictures; What To Do If She Won't Come Out Of The Bathroom; and many more hilariously funny situations newlyweds may encounter.

2067-It's Time To Retire When... Your boss is younger than you are, you stop to think and sometimes forget to start again, or you feel like the morning after and you swear you haven't been anywhere.

2068-Sex Manual For People Over 30. Includes great excuses for nonperformance, rediscovering foreplay, and how to tell an orgasm from a heart attack.

2101-Peter Pecker's Guide To The Male Organ. A detailed analysis of the types of men who own Wee Wee's, Members, Weenies, Dinks, Schlongs, No Nos, Tools, Wangs, and many others. Everyone is covered, from accountants to taxi drivers.

2102-You Know You're Over 50 When... You add "God willing" to the end of most of your statements and you don't care where your wife goes when she goes out, as long as you don't have to go with her. A great 50 year old birthday gift.

2109-The Get Well Book. Cheer up sick folks with this book that teaches them how to gain sympathy, what the doctor really means and how to cope with phones, kids, germs and critters that make you sick.

2121-More Dirty Crosswords. This latest edition of dirty crosswords will test your analytical powers even further as you struggle to improve your vocabulary.

2123-You Know You're Over 60 When... You're 60 when you start straddling two road lanes, you start looking forward to dull evenings at home, and you can't remember when prunes and figs weren't a regular part of your diet.

2127-Your Golf Game Is In Big Trouble When... Your practice rounds are all in the bar and you've tried out 30 putters and none of them work and you play whole rounds without once hitting the fairway.

2129-Fun In The John. More fun than you ever dreamed possible. Crosswords, Bathroom Lists, Word Searches, Mystery Games, John Horoscopes, Connect The Dots, Mazes, and Much More.

2131-The Fart Book. Farts are divided into two groups. 1. Your farts. 2. Somebody else's fart. This book lists them all, the Little Girls Don't Fart Fart, the Dog Did It Fart, the S'cuse me Fart and many more.

2136-The Shit List. The list is quite extensive and describes the versatile use of this clever word. There is, for example, "chicken shit" and "give a shit" and "shoot the shit". A very funny book, No Shit.

2148-Dear Teacher...A hilarious collection of actual parents' notes to teachers. "Please excuse Joe from school yesterday. He had diarrhea through a hole in his shoe."

2153-Fart Part II. This sequel covers the dreaded "Thank God I'm Alone Fart", the insidious "SBD Fart" and the awe-inspiring "Sonic Boom Fart".

2166-You've Survived Catholic School When... You can enter a phone booth without feeling you should begin confessing and you don't shudder when someone hands you a ruler.

2175-Asses. The complete directory of asses of all kinds from the Male Biker's Buns to the Oh Wow! Ass.

2177-You're Over the Hill When... No one cares anymore about what you did in high school, and you see your old cereal bowl in an antique shop.

2178-The Pregnant Father. The Pregnant Father's chief duty during delivery is to hold a little pan while his wife throws up into it...and much more!

2190-Teddy Bears Are Better Than Men Because... They don't hog the whole bed and they invariably understand when you have a headache.

2192-You Know You're Over 30 When... You start wearing underwear almost all of the time; you find the first grey hair and you no longer have to lie on your resume.

2195-Beer Is Better Than Women Because... Beers don't want a lasting relationship, and beer doesn't expect an hour of foreplay before satisfying you.

2198-The P.M.S. Book. What every woman experiences once a month. Includes the Irritability Syndrome, the Tender Boobs Syndrome and the Chocolate Syndrome.

2200-Shit Happens... It happens when the IRS asks for the receipts, your husband leaves you for an older woman, or you call suicide prevention and they put you on hold.

2202-Stressed Out... Being stressed out is trying to enjoy a cigarette in a non-smoking office, or having some kid park your brand new car.

2203-The Last Fart Book. This final sequel concludes with the Under The Cover Fart, the Waiting Room Fart, the Excuses Fart and many others.

2205-Is There Sex After 40? Normal 40-year olds do it once a week. Covers everything from sexy cardigans to tucking a vest into your underpants.

2210- Is There Sex After Marriage? This great work covers everything from faking an orgasm to philandering to excuses for more or less sex. It even answers the age old question, Is There Sex After Pets?

2211- Boobs. Using the Standard Boob as a benchmark, this screamer examines the Pillow Boobs, Star Gazers, Spreaders, Ninnies, Disappearing Boobs, Oh Wow! Boobs and 40 others.

2212- Life With A Sports Junky. The Sports Junky spent part of his honeymoon in a grandstand, still asks his old coach for advice and thinks sex is O.K. as long as it is over by game time.

2213- Women Over 50 Are Better... They can tune out the worst snoring, have more womanly figures & won't make you sleep in the middle of a stuffed animal collection.

2214-Is There Sex After Divorce? All the funny situations when a middle aged person starts to date again, from not fooling around on the first date to finding a zit on your date's ear.

2215-Over 65, The Golden Years? Great birthday and retirement gift. Describes "Bellies Are Beautiful", Early Bird Dinners", "Retirement, What Now?" and much more.

2216-Hanky Panky. Cartoons of the animal kingdom in their favorite amorous (and unmentionable) pastime. Brilliant full color drawings are riotously funny.

2217-Is There Sex After 50? Swapping your mate for two 25-year-olds, finding places to put your cold feet, and telling grandchildren about when you were a hippy.

2218-Is There Sex After 60? Searching, in depth, cartoon report into the sexual behavior and horrible habits of the Don Juans of the Geriatric set. The Sewing Circle Seductress matches wits with the Casanovas of the Bingo Halls.

2219-Crosswords For Shitheads. For that person you feel is full of "it".

2220-Crosswords For Farters. A crossword puzzle book for people with gastrointestinal distress.

2221-Crosswords For Your Birthday. An irreverent crossword puzzle book for people who are terribly lonesome on their birthday.

2222-Crosswords For Bored Lovers. Designed to test you and your partner's sexual knowledge (or lack of it). Grab your lover, think sex, and dive in.

2223-Games You Can't Lose. An exciting way to test your skills and increase your self-confidence with puzzles, mazes, word searches, and many more games.

2224-Life's A Picnic If You Have A Big Weenie. Covers where big weenies come from, what women like about big weenies, making a teenie weenie into a big weenie, and much more.

2225-Women Over 40 Are Better Because... They know just what it takes to make their man feel good and they can eat a double hot fudge sundae and not worry about "breaking out".

2226-C.R.S. (Can't Remember Shit). It happens to the best of us like forgetting the punch line of a great joke, where you parked the car, or where you left your glasses.

2227-Happy Birthday! You Know You're A Year Older When... You no longer eat all the dessert just because it's there and you can no longer easily sleep till noon.

2228-You're Hooked On Fishing When... You start to raise your own worms, you visit the emergency room at least once a year to have a hook removed, and you're on a first name basis with the Coast Guard.

2229-You Know You're A Redneck When... You wear bib overalls, eat grits, love cow tipping, and think a mud wrestling place is hog heaven.

2230-A Coloring Book for Pregnant Mothers To Be. Tender and funny, from being unable to see the scale to controlling your proud parents.

2231-Eating Pussy The Official Cat Cookbook. This book will not only offer you great new ideas for serving pussy to your guests, but it is sure to expand your recipe file.

2232-Life's More Fun When You're 21... This book humorously covers the trials of coming of age such as parental trust, joining the work force, and balancing budgets.

2233-Small Busted Women Are Better Because. Finally a book that boasts the benefits of being small busted in our society where bigger is better! A super way to bolster the ego of every slender woman.

TRADE BOOKS - $7.00 Postpaid

2400-How To Have Sex On Your Birthday. Finding a partner, special birthday sex position, places to keep your birthday erection, faking the birthday orgasm and much more.

2401-Is There Sex After Children? There are chapters on pre-teens and privacy, keeping toddlers out of your bedroom, places to hide lingerie, where children come from, things kids bring to show and tell and more.

2402-Confessions From The Bathroom. The Gas Station Dump, for example, the Porta Pottie Dump, the Sunday Newspaper Dump to mention just a few.

2403-The Good Bonking Book. Bonking is a great new British term for doing "you know what". Covers bonking in the dark, bonking all night long, improving your bonking and everything else you've ever wanted (or maybe didn't want) to know.

2404-Sex Slave:How To Find One, How To Be One. What it takes to be a Sex Slave, how to pick up Sex Slaves, the fine art of groveling and more than you ever imagined.

2405-Mid-Life Sex. Taking all night to do what you used to do all night and having biological urges dwindle to an occasional nudge.

2406-World's Sex Records. Lists the greatest records of all time, including the kinkiest bedroom, the greatest sex in a car, most calories burned during sex, plus many more.

2407-40 Happens. You realize anyone with the energy to do it on a weeknight must be a sex maniac.

2408-30 Happens. You take out a life-time membership at your health club and you still wonder when the baby fat will finally disappear.

2409-50 Happens. When you can't remember what you went to the top of the stairs for and when 'made in Japan' meant something that didn't work.

2410-Bosom Buddies. Uncovered at last--the truth about women's bouncy parts: they're probably talking to each other! This book tells us what they would say, if only we could hear them!

2411-Geriatric Sex Guide. It's not his mind that needs expanding, and you're in the mood now, but by the time you're naked, you won't be!

2412-Golf Shots. Humorously tells you how to look for lost balls, what excuses to use to play through first, ways to distract your opponent, and where and when a true golfer is willing to play golf.

2413-101 Ways To Improve Your Husband Or Wife. How to make your husband or wife more romantic, improve their taste in clothing, increase their sexual appetite, and to create a more meaningful relationship.